FORBIDDEN DEMAND

—·—

Book 1

Phoenix Skyy

Mind Flow Publishing & Production LLC

This book or any portion thereof may not be reproduced or used in any manner whatsoever without the publisher's express written permission except for the use of brief quotations in a book review or scholarly journal.

This is a work of fiction. Names, characters, businesses, places, events, locales, and incidents are either the products of the author's imagination or used in a fictitious manner. Any resemblances to actual persons, living or dead, or actual events are purely coincidental.

Additional copies of this book and others are available by mail.

Mind Flow Publishing & Production LLC

PO Box 48768 Cumberland, North Carolina 28331-8768

by visiting the website listed below.

Check the website for pricing.

www.mindflowpublishingproduction.com

Cover Design by RJ Creatives

Formatting by Carlette Whitlock

Copyright © 2023 Phoenix Skyy

Mind Flow Publishing & Production LLC

ISBN PAPERBACK 978-1-951271-75-6

ISBN EBOOK 978-1-951271-90-9

FORBIDDEN DEMAND

All rights reserved

Contents

Dedication	VI
Prologue	VII
1. Chapter One	1
2. Chapter Two	17
3. Chapter Three	27
4. Chapter Four	37
5. Chapter Five	47
6. Chapter Six	53
7. Chapter Seven	63
8. Chapter Eight	77
9. Chapter Nine	93
Acknowledgments	101
Also By	102
Also By	103

A special dedication to all of my family and my friends.

Thank you for being by my side.

Thank you to God for guiding my path

Prologue

27 Years Ago

Cory's eyes fly open, her heart threatening to beat straight out of her chest. Her body still on edge, she was unsure if this was this only another nightmare seeping into reality. But no — she could still hear it, even as her vision adjusted, and the sobering reality of her life took hold. There's nothing quite as unsettling as hearing a child cry in the middle of the night when you live alone. There was something strange about this baby's wails. They were thick, gnarled — animalistic, almost. It would send chills down the spine of any ordinary person, but Cory wasn't ordinary.

As the guttural crying continues, Cory props herself up. *A cub?* "Couldn't be..." whispering to herself, Cory slips on her robe and tiptoes to her door.

She isn't in the safest part of the city, but whatever danger may be lurking outside, she knew she had to at least make sure the fussing child was alright. Peeking through the solid oak door's peephole, she sees only darkness and the flickering streetlights. She had a theory; as to why the lights were never replaced on this side of town. People in the city disregarded the assaults of the poor. Hands shaking, Cory knows this could be a trap. There could be a full-grown shifter waiting for her just around the corner, using their child as bait. She gingerly opens the door, and her eyes look around and follow the loud wailing — no wonder it sounded as if it was in her home! The child was right at her door. Wrapped in a pink crocheted blanket was a baby with patches of fur shifting in and out of her delicate skin.

"That must hurt," she whispers. Shifting the first time was painful for any panther, but a newborn? Her skin pricked with tiny bits of blood each time. "You poor thing!" Cory picks up the baby, scanning to see if there are any signs of who left her before heading inside.

"Why would your pack drop you off here?" she coos. A panther? Panthers are the elite shifters.... Surely this cub had better places she could go, but they chose this neighborhood. Her? Cory did have a reputation for looking after the shifters, but a panther, it made such little sense.

The baby shakes as it continues to shift. Another strange occurrence. Babies hardly ever shift. In fact, most shifters don't even experience their first shift until their teenage years. It's often brought on by intense trauma. "I suppose this must be quite traumatic," she whispers. "Don't worry. I'll cover all of these wounds with love, little heart." She kisses where the tufts of fur kept poking out, as the baby relaxed under her toughness. "You'll not remember this soon enough."

Chapter One

Nette

Present Day

Every birthday I can remember, my mother has ensured it was the most special day. It didn't matter if we didn't have money or if the other kids were making a fuss about how mom treats me "better", she made sure I had a cake, gifts, and even took my brothers away to remind them that I am not like them. "Nette has a birthday wound," she'd say, "and every time her day comes, it hurts. It's a unique wound." The older we got, the more they knew of my story and could understand that I was not their birth sister. I was abandoned at the steps of their mother's door long before they were born.

A large oak door, solid enough to keep intruders out, and I can't help but wonder on days like today — did my mom touch it with her hand? Did she try to knock first before leaving me here? And why did she abandon me? My 'birthday wound' aches more with each passing year.

Now, my brothers — Lawrence and Angel — are working tirelessly in the kitchen to help mom make my favorite birthday dinner and a beautiful cake. Mom's older now and gone are the days when she could pipe elaborate frosting and design cakes that would make even the most popular bakers on those reality TV shows jealous. Now, she grows frustrated with all the things she can't do because of the rheumatoid arthritis that wrecks her body and has distorted her hands. "Cory!" a man bellows, as he walks into the kitchen. "Let me do this!"

I look up and see Tommy's warm smile. He's a 'boarder', as Mom calls them. I'm not her only 'rescue' — as I call us. He takes the whisk from her hand and orders her to sit by me. When she does, I wink. "Don't worry. It's not *that* bad being forced to do nothing."

She laughs and wraps her arm around me. "How are you already twenty-seven? You're practically —"

"Shh! Don't say it. We don't speak that number here. Not on this holy day." I tease.

"She's right though. You're getting to be old, Nette! When are you going to find yourself a man to settle down with?" Tommy asks, his hands whisking away.

I always think about how I want to buy Mom one of those fancy Kitchen Aids mixers, but I've never been able to keep a job long enough. I have so many obstacles in my way, from the color of my skin to the size of my wallet to where I live… and in my community, the community of shifters, I am a taboo. A panther. I should be on the upper east side, living with the elite, with the rest of my kind… but apparently, even they didn't want me. I try not to let these thoughts weigh me down today, because I know how much effort my mother puts into this day — my entire family and even our neighbors, but for some reason this one, 27? It hits differently.

Maybe it's the whole 27 Club theory because deep down I never thought I'd make it past 26. Mom showered me with so much love and I had the best life, but as much as she tried to tend to wounds, she never left. She couldn't heal them. I couldn't either. As a teenager, it consumed me, and the idea of living this long once sounded like a nightmare.

Yet here I am. With the best family anyone could ask for...

"Why don't you two go and do a little shopping, hm?" Tommy sits down a gift card, beaming. It's $50 and his bright smile almost brings me to tears. "Don't worry! It's legit. I worked hard for it. I know, I know. I should be saving for myself, but I wanted to say thank you."

Mom stands up and pulls him into a hug. "Tommy, remember to treat yourself too."

"Ah," he dismisses her. "You guys 'treat' me all the time. Enjoy."

"When you two get back, the party will be ready to start." Tommy does a little dance.

My brother chimes in, "Just come back at four, okay? We got to get some extra special surprises ready."

"Got it!"

Looping my arm through my mother's, we made our way to the car. It's a 2005 Chevy Malibu, bright red, and not at all fitting for either of our personalities, but it was cheap and well... it works. It gets us from point A to point B, which right now is the mall.

"Don't you dare spend a penny of that on me," she insists before I even start the car.

"I wasn't going —"

"I know you, hun. You would buy me a present on your birthday with your birthday money."

"Well, he did kind of say it was for both of us." I run my fingers through my hair, clicking the key fob and hearing its satisfying beep and click. It was only a few years ago we had a car so old it did not have a key fob and even the windows had to be rolled down manually.

She sighs. "I have all I could ever want." Her brown eyes brim with tears, and there's something strange about the way she says it.

"Is everything okay, Mom?" I ask, my heart fluttering with an unfamiliar fear.

"Of course, sweetie. It always is."

Our shopping trip ends up being a game of me trying to sneak Mom a little something special while her stopping me at every turn, but I finally manage to get her to agree to a buy one get one deal on a pair of shoes. We are both in need of a new pair of boots for the upcoming winter, and even Mom can't refuse a deal like that!

We stop to get lemonades on the way out before we head back home.

I am twisting the doorknob, knowing immediately there'll be a grand affair the moment I step in. Well, the grandest my neighborhood will ever see, but I did not expect the beauty that awaits me. Gasping, I can't even form words. Mom is speechless too! "Are those fresh flowers?" she asks. She's right. They are. Fresh daisies. Everywhere.

"I have connections." Tommy winks.

All of our boarders have connections — often not good ones, but Tommy is one of those people who makes friends with everyone. Good and bad. I smiled and ran up to give him a big hug. "Thank you." My brothers immediately began chiming in where they helped, just like they did as children. Not much has changed. I laugh and give them both hugs, too.

Mom stubbornly carries out the birthday cake, candles lit and all. I pray her hands hold it in place, for her sake. All of us seem to hold our breath before she snaps at us to start singing. "I'm not going to drop it!" We laugh, and everyone begins to sing and when I blow out the candles, I find myself wishing for something I don't have yet:

Love.

I have a family, yes. But even the greatest family can't replace what I deeply long for most — someone to love me.

As if the Universe immediately grants me my wish, my Angel declares he has a surprise for me. "A blind date!"

I audibly gag. "A what?" This is *not* what I meant! Sure, I want to find someone but someone my brothers picked out? On my birthday, no less? No thanks.

"I... Is he here?" I ask, looking around.

He roars. "Goodness no! You're a hard sale in this crowd," he teases, and everyone laughs. Mom pats my shoulder. "But I go to Church with him in the next town over. You know that one I've been visiting lately? Well, he's a good man, and I didn't want to invite him to your birthday, but... we're meeting him at Moonlight and Rivers Theatre."

"How on earth are we going to afford that?"

Mom immediately chastises me. "We have guests. Be grateful, Nette."

This is too much! I mean, do I like being spoiled? Sure. As much as the next girl. But this? Moonlight and Rivers Theatre isn't a theater at all. It's a nightclub on the upper east side. You get in either with money or fame, which is basically the same thing when you think about it. We had neither. Unless my date...

"Your date was kind enough to invite us there."

I blush and apologize. How rude can I be? Assumptive much? I sigh. Everyone quickly forgets about my little faux pas, and they move on to eating the cake, declaring how delicious it is, and congratulating my mother for her perfect baking skills. I noticed the sadness on her face that she wasn't the one to bake it this time. It was her recipe, but she had help... something, like me, she didn't like having. Even if she was so quick to help others.

When a limo picks us up, I ask my brother Lawrence where exactly he found this man — and speaking of that man, where the hell was he? "He's at the club. Waiting for us," my brother Lawrence answers, popping open the courtesy champagne bottle.

"What exactly is this church you've been going to out of town?"

He laughs. "It's where the rich folk go."

I nod. Obviously. Part of me is excited to see who this mystery man is. It's such an unusual experience for me, and as annoyed as I am, I'm intrigued. The other part of me? I am almost wondering if my brother isn't just enjoying the benefits of me being dolled upon... I mean, he and my other brother are tagging along as well.

Despite being eyed suspiciously — clearly, we don't fit this scene — the moment we drop the name 'Tanner Richardson', the bouncer lets us in immediately. Jay leads us through the crowd, on his cellphone, following directions until we're standing in front of what is a reasonably attractive man, but I can tell almost immediately that I hate him. Okay, hate is a strong word

— but the way his eyes are eating up the other girls around us? Why am I even here?

Tanner greets him with a firm handshake, and it all feels very formal and business-like. "Nice to meet you. Sorry about my brother here," I joke. "He thought a human for a birthday present would one up everyone else."

Tanner laughs, but he doesn't seem amused. Another man sitting next to him, however, does. His deep laughter echoes throughout my body. "Noah," he introduces himself, and my body is afire with him, taking notice of me. It's as if it's just the two of us in the room.

Blushing, I offer my name. "Jeanette. But everyone calls me Nette."

I quickly learn that Tanner is an investor who likes to do nothing more than talk about himself. When my brothers have left the bar to go dance and do what it is you'd think I should also be doing at a nightclub on my birthday, we sit talking about numbers while he looks on at the scantily dressed women. It's as if I am not here. Not really.

Suddenly, I feel a warm hand over mine. Looking up, perplexed — Tanner is still beside me. One hand on his drink and the other picking up his greasy food — I notice immediately it's Noah. "Would you like to dance?"

I start to ask Tanner if he'd mind when Noah interrupts. "He won't notice. Come on."

Just as his laughter filled my body with desire, the energy of dancing with him, the way his skin presses against mine, and the flirtatious grin whenever he notices a shiver course through me, sends me to a place I forgot even existed in me. I want him. I want Noah. Do I know him? No. Will I ever see him again after this? Also, no. Do I care? Not tonight.

Before I know it we're slipping away from the crowd into a private room that I can only assume exists just for this — for what I want. I've never had sex with a stranger before. I'm not that kind of girl, but tonight isn't a normal kind of night. Something about Noah feels electric, magnetic. I need him. Our lips are interlocked, my hands tugging at his clothes. Why is he dressed in a goddamn suit? I groan in frustration, causing him to laugh. He's already removed most of my clothes.

"Allow me," he purrs. He commands me to sit on the sofa in the room. I start to refuse — I never much liked someone telling me what to do. "Obey me," he pleads firmly.

I immediately fell into place. Removing his clothes, I am taken aback by his beauty. A strong, masculine beauty. He is fierce. Commanding. Smooth. Elegant. His eyes were golden, inquisitive, and knowing. It's as if he sees past my naked body into something even rawer. Me. The no one else ever sees. As if he can see my deepest desires.

He slowly stalks toward me in a way that can only be described as feline, and for a brief moment, I wonder if he is a shifter. He is taunting me, knowing how badly I want him. I try not to show my frustration, but when he laughs again; I know it's obvious. He pounces on me. Our lips connected once again, his fingers going right to where I need him most.

I moan his name as if it's the most familiar word in the world. As if I've known him, his body, my whole life. Circling my clit, he takes my nipples in his mouth, his erection grazing my leg. *Oh my. This is going to be nice.* My hips arch, anticipating being filled with him. I reach and grab his cock firmly. He pulls away from my breast, letting out a deep moan. Stroking each other, I slowly lead him where I want him to be.

He bites my neck, nibbles my ear, and all of it is overwhelming my senses. I've never had someone take so much time, care, slowly teasing me with their body. Someone so in control of their own body. When he comes inside, I gasp and grab his hips, pulling him deeper.

"You're beautiful," he whispers. "And far more intelligent than any of the other *ones* here."

Ones? Does he know I'm a shifter? Does he mean girls? But I can't even think anymore, because the moment he says that I can feel him pick up the pace, his hands cupping my breast, and my body takes over. Responding. All that exists is us.

He pulls my hair, and I swear his nails grow longer as they dig into my skin. The pain and pleasure mixing and sending me over the edge. "Noah," I cry out, my hips riding him faster.

"That's it," he purrs. "Take what's yours."

And so I do — and god does it feel good. My body shivering into his as if my pleasure is enough to give him what he needs, he falls into me, crying out my name in release.

Chapter Two

Noah

"Nette!" I moan, collapsing onto her body. Licking her thighs and moving my way back up to her lips, I pause. "We'll have to do this again sometime." I purr, caressing her breasts, teasing her one last time.

As I get dressed, she observes me. "Happy birthday, Nette." I said coolly and left her alone. I make it back to our table first. Tanner doesn't even seem to notice either of us left as he continues to boast about himself. Her brothers, however, took notice and looked at me with a clear warning. I can't help but wonder what a shifter like her is doing with the likes of them. I have half a mind to ask, but Nette returns and slips back into her place.

She holds up her hand, signaling one of the blondes my father employs to come to us. "What can I get you?" the server asks.

"Can I get a shot of tequila?"

She is flustered. It's fucking adorable. "I'll take one too," I say seductively, my eyes focused on Nette.

The server nearly drops her tray. "Y... Yes, of course."

"Did I miss something?" Tanner asks.

"No!" Nette blanches. "Nothing at all. Tell me, what was that method you said you were implementing with that program at work?"

Tanner immediately falls into a dull speech, and I have to wonder — will I ever see this magical woman again?

I tap my pen, much to my father's annoyance, as he does his best to deliver what is meant to be a motivational speech, but it really comes across as a lecture about how terrible everyone is. I smile apologetically at those across the table the moment Dad looks at his notes. I used to wonder if he wrote "chastise employees" or "criticize Kerri's hairstyle" on them. I am sure everyone else here wonders the same, but I know they think I'm just like him. I wish there was a way to let them know I'm on their side.

Sure, I have the privilege of being both a member of the Midnight Shadows Pack, a group of panther shifters and the son of Rob Kahan, the CEO of MidnightZ. But I was far from favored, especially by my father. If these people here only knew my dad ripped me a new one several times a day — only he did it in the privacy of his own office or our family home and not in the once-a-week meetings.

"MidnightZ shouldn't be suffering this quarter!" his father flails his hands. "I mean, what the fuck are these numbers? Hm?"

I flinch. Hasn't he heard of tact? Gen Z would have a field day with his abusive language in our meetings. MidnightZ is the biggest umbrella company for both shifters and humans, spanning nightclubs, record labels, and the unofficial political structure for shifters in the area.

It was exactly as sketchy as it sounded, but it was all I've ever known. And besides, we did a lot of good. We kept shifters in line. We kept our kind out of the limelight. We kept those shifters, who would rather be reckless in their place.

With an exasperated sigh that sounds more like a dog whining, my father interrupts my dissociative spell. "Never mind any of this! I have news."

News? I haven't heard any news. "What news?"

"Some of you know, I have expressed a deep interest in becoming involved in human politics."

That's news to me. I cock my head. Where exactly is this going? I knew my dad expressed interest, but he's not said anything beyond wanting to get his hands in it *one day*. He's been so caught up with MidnightZ and our own internal political system. Humans like to keep things separate — especially things they don't understand, things they view as less than others. While the majority of society is not aware of us, many of the human elite are. And some unlucky humans who are subject to foul types like wolf packs that are careless with their interactions.

"Well," I say, as my dad continues his silence.

"Well, don't act surprised." He laughs, pointing over at me. "My son, always a great pretender! Now that I am running for mayor, I will need to step down from my position as MidnightZ CEO. Stand up, Noah! Everyone, I want you to meet your new CEO. Noah!"

I blink. And I keep blinking as if somehow the surrounding scene will change.

I did not agree with this.

I would've never agreed to this!

"What the actual fuck, Dad?" I scream the moment we are alone in his soundproof office, a feature I wasn't sure was about our fights or his sexual escapades — a fact I loathe to even acknowledge. My mother is an amazing and strong woman, but shifters — especially panthers — are notorious for being non-monogamous.

"Oh, come on, son. It was an obvious choice. You would've said yes, anyway."

"If that's the case, why didn't you ask? Or even let me know."

"You're welcome," he says, drawing out each syllable. It's as if he truly believes this is a gift.

"How is Tessa doing?" he asks. "I haven't seen her around for a while. She'd make a lovely secretary. I mean, you can keep your old one."

"They're not property." I correct him. "And Tessa and I broke up. Besides, I would never work with someone I'm..."

"Fucking?"

"If that's what you want to call it." He is right. That's exactly what Tessa, and I were doing. I know my father is all about sexual expression, but he's also about settling down and keeping the panther bloodline continuing. Something I'll do when I'm older. It's not as if I don't have time!

"Is that what you were doing with that girl at the club last night? Who was she?"

I shake my head. "What does that matter?"

"Was she at least one of us?"

I nod. "Yes. I hadn't seen her before this, but I could feel it. I even saw her claws." I blush the moment the words are out. Dammit. I do my best to keep what few boundaries I can in place with my parents — especially my father.

"Well, at least she was one of us."

I nod, wondering what he'd think if he knew the people with her were not our kind. I couldn't quite place their smell, but I knew they weren't panthers and weren't entirely human either.

"You're right though. I've never seen her either. Get her name next time, will you? If she's new to town, we should welcome her properly." Dad looks at his phone, smiles, and looks back up at me. "By the way, Tessa is actually going to be working with you to help me with my campaign."

"You're what? I will not be —"

"Let her in," my father says through his little intercom. I realize that soon this will be my office, and suddenly the responsibilities that soon face me fill my mind, just as the door swings open and Tessa stands before me.

"Noah darling!" she squeals.

I cringe.

Why did I ever think she was fuckable?

Tessa and I immediately began working on my dad's campaign. I sit in front of a computer beside a designer, giving directions for mockup campaign posters while Tessa works with the copywriter to create the perfect slogan. She is annoying as hell, but she can be just as creative — I'll give her that. In reality, I suppose it was how she marketed herself that made me think she was fuckable. A worthwhile thrill.

Anxiously, I keep glancing at my phone, hoping to see a text from the mystery panther. Each time Tessa' tries to flirt with me, I hardly notice, because all I can see is the mystery girl's breasts, her shoulders, her eyes, hips — everything, and it's as if I can feel myself against her skin.

"Can you focus, Mr. CEO? If your dad doesn't win, you won't be taking over the business, you know?"

I frown. "As if I want to."

"What?" she gasps.

Shit. I didn't mean to say that out loud. "Nothing. Let's get this done."

"You and your daddy issues." She laughs. "I'd be annoyed if it wasn't so damned cute."

"Please keep this professional, Tessa," I respond curtly.

She sighs just as my phone goes off.

Ding

I grabbed my phone. It's her. She texted! "I have to take this." I excuse myself.

My body is overflowing with a need so deep that before I even look at the full text, I allow myself one last moment of indulgence — after all, if this is but an illusion it could come crashing down the moment, I read a possible rejection text. Alone now in my office, I gently caress my cock, already throbbing with need. And just like all day today, I see her - her lips, hips, and breasts as I imagine Nette on her knees pleasing me.

"Goddammit."

CHAPTER THREE

NETTE

I stare at my phone and the number Noah put in there — I could text him... I could do it, but why? Once he knows who I am and that I didn't truly belong in MidnightZ, would he even want to see me again? Wiping the sleep from my eyes, I toss my phone across the room. "No, I am not letting a man rule my life!" I declare aloud.

Slipping on my favorite fuzzy robe, hungover from my birthday celebrations, I am immediately appalled by the smell of bacon and eggs. "Really, Mom?" I murmur.

"Hey!" She waves her spatula. "No one told you to drink an entire bar, Nette!"

I frown. "I didn't. I just had a bit more than usual." That's because my usual is less than a glass of wine on most occasions, but I don't say that. Instead, I gladly take the water and medicine my brother hands me.

Nette wants to text Noah, but she knows he is way out of her league. Once he knows she doesn't belong in that club, he'll want nothing to do with her and that's for the best, because she is already fighting against rich men like him.

It's no secret the system — both the human system and the shifter system — is built in such a way to keep the rich and elite in their esteemed positions while the rest of us try to claw our ways to the top, but it's only an illusion. We can't reach the top. We're chained to the ground. Those of us who have fought long enough and hard enough to know this. We've seen all our efforts fail us. As a panther shifter, someone who should be an elite, living in poverty, I am in a unique position.

I manage to stuff down a few bites of eggs and sip my orange juice, opting for another cup of coffee before I head out to my job. It's not so much of a job as a volunteer gig with a non-profit my mother and I started a few years back, Shifting Resources. It's how Mom finds most of her boarders — people we can't place or find space for, but we're overflowing... I can only imagine what will happen when our grant runs out.

It's easy not to think about Noah at work, but it's not a good thing. Sitting in front of me is a human and in her arms is a baby. A baby shifter mixed just like me. It's not often we get cases that hit this close to home, and when we do, someone else is usually around to take over for us — but today has been chaotic. With the ominous announcement that Rob Kahan, an elite shifter, is running for office in the city, the entire office has been eerily unsettled. Rob is someone who has fought hard to keep our non-profit restricted to one location. In fact, he is the reason our grant from the Shifter Authorities was limited. We can't register and receive funds from humans — it's too complicated, and how on earth could I explain a situation like the one I face right now?

"Mandy," I say, placing my hand over hers. "I know this must be so hard for you. I mean, you had no idea what you were signing up for."

"I didn't even know shifters existed," she cries, her head hanging low. "I love her. I do. But I can't keep up with her needs. She eats so much, and she is growing faster than the other babies. I heard that's normal... but I just can't keep up. And what do I do when she does finally shift?"

I nod. For a brief moment, I realized how traumatizing it must have been when my own birth mother watched me shifting, a rare occurrence. "We have resources," I offer. "We can supply the extra food you need. There are also counseling options for both you and your daughter. Of course, we are here to support any choice you make. There are many shifter families that would be happy to adopt a pup." I cringe as I catch myself using the slang for a baby were-shifter. "What I mean to say," careful to use the appropriate language, "if you choose to place your daughter, we would be happy to coordinate the adoption." I go on to explain open-and-closed adoptions and when the young woman in front of me breathes a sigh of relief, I know her answer.

I see the hurt in her eyes, and I know this isn't easy. I refer her to our therapist on staff. Just as Mandy leaves, my brother Lawrence rushes in. "I just got off work! You could've rescheduled for one of us to meet with her..." he says, looking after Mandy's silhouette as she exits the building.

"I have to face my past at some point." I swipe away the tears I feel finally spill now that it's only us. "I've been blaming my birth mother this entire time... but this woman... she fell in love with a shifter who didn't even tell her who he was. Then he left the moment she got pregnant... and her baby isn't even shifting early like I did.... She just can't afford to keep up with her needs. She had no idea shifters existed. She lost everything. I would do the same."

He listens silently, waiting for me to reach my conclusion. I love that about him. He never hovers or pressures me when it comes to this topic. I continue, "I think I want to find my birth mom. But we can't let Mom know. Not yet. Would you help me?"

He nods carefully. "Of course, Nette. Are you sure you want this?"

"Yes."

"Okay, well, now that we have this serious shit out of the way. Tell me about that guy last night. Did he text you back yet?"

I frown. "I haven't texted him."

"You what!" He nearly screeches. "Nette. He gave you his number! Text him. Now." He reaches for my phone on the desk and sits there until I type a quick message, my heart pounding.

Hey Noah. This is Nette from the club last night. You gave me your number? I had a great time and well maybe we should meet up again.

Before I hit send, I looked up at him. "Are you sure we want to do this? I mean, he's one of them — a rich guy... The reason we're all here."

"Nette. This could be your way out."

I growl. "I would never let a man support me."

"Just do it."

I think about his body and the magnetic pull between us, my cheeks turning red. I press send.

"See, it wasn't that hard, was it?"

I roll my eyes, tossing my phone into my purse. "Time to go to the real job," I declare. This meant I would have to lock my phone away the moment I hit the call floor and continued the rest of my day as a 911 operator — a job I both loved and loathed. It paid well, but it took such a toll and I often blame myself for when things go wrong on a call... even if I am not the one there to save them, if it's not my fault.

Time goes by slowly because there are fewer calls today, something I should be grateful for, but all I can think of is checking my phone.

Just when I am about to clock out for my lunch break, a call comes in. A big one. "Help! Please help. There's something chasing me."

"Okay miss, what is chasing you?"

"It's like a dog. But bigger. Or maybe it's a big cat... Yeah, it's a cat."

"Like a mountain lion?" Nette's blood runs cold.

"Bigger."

"Where are you?" Nette asks. For a moment, she is hesitant to send help. What if it's one of her kind?

"Nowhere near a zoo!" the girl screams. "I'm on campus. The library." She rattles off an address.

"Is anyone else there with you?" Surely, the library isn't empty. Nette begins to wonder if this is a prank call, but the girl goes silent.

There is a growl — and it reminds her so much of Noah. "Are you okay? Answer me! I am sending someone right away."

There's more screaming and then what sounds like yelling. "How could you? This isn't funny! I was literally on the phone with the police." More laughter echoes through Nette's headset. "Shit! I'm still on the line with them."

"I am so sorry. My friends were dressed in a weird cat suit chasing me around for some college prank."

I ran through a series of questions and told the girl that we still have police on the way, explaining that its procedure to ensure everyone is indeed safe.

"Of course." As the girl giggles, I have half a mind to lecture them, but she clicks off. Before I can take my lunch or put myself in after-call, another call comes pouring in. Dammit. All I want to do is check my phone.

After what feels like a decade, my lunch break finally comes — I barely answer my coworker's questions about my birthday, briefly mumbling something about going to

MidnightZ. I open my phone. There is a notification. A thrill runs through me when I see that it's Noah. I'm scared to open it, but I can hear my brother's voice urging me to just give it a shot.

After all, what can it hurt? And if the worst was another blissful night like last night, well, sign me up!

So, I embrace this new side of me, and I open his text message and read it:

I would love that. How about we talk a bit first this time? How does dinner tonight sound?

I almost squeal. My co-worker eyes my curiously. "A boy?" she asks.

"A man," I correct, and I hate how cheesy it sounds, but goddamn, if they knew what being with Noah was like, they wouldn't dare call him a boy.

Chapter Four

Noah

Hours pass before Nette answers me again — grateful that I gave myself a moment to release the built-up tension of the day — and I begin to wonder if she perhaps has changed her mind. I am sipping on a dark caramel liquid when I hear my phone go off.

Yes. Of course, she hasn't changed her mind. Who could after the night we had? She agrees to dinner but refuses to let me pick her up. Strange. It's not as if we haven't met yet. Of course, we met under very different circumstances. I drop the name of my favorite restaurant and say we'll meet at nine. She only sends a thumbs up. Also, strange. Most women are falling over themselves for me.

Before leaving the office, I asked one of the office assistants if she's heard of a panther shifter named Nette. "Or any variation of that? Like Janette?" I add for good measure.

She frowns. "I mean, there are some older ones. Like... your mom's age..." *Great. Now she thinks I'm into women my mom's age.*

"Thank you." I cut her short.

"What's this?" I hear Tessas' voice chime in. *Really?* I figured she had left when I stormed home for my lunch.

"Didn't you leave yet?" I growl.

In any other work setting, this might be considered hostile and land me with a lawsuit. But shifters? The rules didn't apply to us. Especially as panthers.

"I was hoping we could get dinner after work," she replies.

"No," I cut her short. "I have plans."

"Oh, come on. I am sure it's nothing you can't reschedule. I mean, I think we should celebrate. You're a CEO now."

I huff. "The paperwork isn't official."

"Your father already announced his interest, and it's going to be official soon. Come on. Besides, I have something extra special to give you —"

"Tessa, stop!" I cut her off before she tells me what this 'special' gift is. I already have a good idea, and hers isn't the body I want tonight. "I do not want to go to dinner with you now or ever. I didn't even want you as my assistant. You have to know that, Tessa?"

She looks me in the eye, daring me to continue. I do.

"My father is the one who hired you for this position. Now, please. I have a date."

"With this Nette chick?" she snaps.

"Yes, actually. I have a date with Nette."

"Is she the chick from the club everyone is talking about?" Tessa pouts.

Of course, my dad received his intel from the gossip. "Tessa," I warn. Her shoulders slouch.

"You're gonna be Alpha soon too, you know? This isn't just about being CEO of MidnightZ. You're destined to take over the pack, Noah. You'll have to find yourself a mate soon."

"Maybe so, but it doesn't have to be you. You're the last shifter I'd willingly select as a mate. So, you and my father can stop. Whatever this little game you two have going, it isn't going to work. No matter how much you push us together, my interests lie elsewhere."

Nette stands outside the restaurant in what can only be described as a vintage dress, but it's adorned with jewels, and so is her hair. It's a unique style, but classy and I can appreciate it. Her hands are twisting, and I immediately hate that I am late. Did she think I was standing her up?

When she sees me, her eyes light up before quickly blushing. I extended my hand immediately and greeted her with a warm side hug. "It's so good to see you again. I wasn't sure if we would." I comment, leading us inside the restaurant.

"Name?" a lady asks when we enter.

"Yes, a reservation for two. Noah Kahan."

She nods, types away on her computer before grabbing two menus and leading us to our table. I notice Nette has been silent the entire time. "Do you go to MidnightZ often?" I ask.

She looks up at me, her eyes suddenly clear, and she sucks in a deep breath. "Actually, can I be brutally honest?"

Shit. What is she about to say? Is she another woman sent to me by my father? Was this all a ploy?

I nod and I brace myself for the worst. "I wouldn't have it any other way. Us Kahans appreciate honesty." *At least this Kahan does*, I almost add.

Her gaze falls. "What did you say?"

"It's okay, to be honest."

"Kahan..." She chews my last name like it's a bitter pill she can't get out of her mouth. "Are you related to Rob?"

"Yep! Good ole dad." I laugh. I wait for her to tell me that she was sent to her by my father, but she looks genuinely perplexed and disappointed. Squinting my brows, I start to piece something together. "You don't know who I am, do you?"

She shakes her head. "I didn't... but I do now... and I think this is all a big mistake..." Nette goes to stand up, and I can't believe this! We barely shared a few words, and she was already running away. What gives? Something in me screams that this is my last chance, but for what, I do not know.

I grabbed her arm. "Sit. Please." I command.

She hesitates. "Fine."

I released her arm and apologized. This is not how I planned the night to go. "I take it you're not a fan?" I asked, frowning. That's a new one. If anything, I spent time fighting off women who exhibited intense fan behavior.

"I was going to be honest with you, and I suppose I still will. I'm not like you. I mean, I am a..." she paused to whisper, "panther like you. But I am not part of your community. I don't have money like you. I don't live in this city. When you saw me at MidnightZ? That was my first time there, and I only got in because of my brother's friend."

I process each word she says, and it's oddly a relief. Confusing — how is she a panther, but not from here? "What pack do you belong to?" I ask skeptically.

"Lone City Wanderers," she answers coolly.

"That's a mixed pack," I note. That explains her 'brothers'...

"Of rejects," she finishes.

"Now, how on earth could you be a 'reject'?"

She blinks at me. "That's a story for another time. I told myself I'd give you a chance, and well, if you still want to give me a chance, why don't we order?"

I smile and summon the waitress.

The rest of dinner went more smoothly than I expected after the rough start. I quickly learn that Nette is the co-owner of a non-profit that helps shifters in need, which

I find admirable. In fact, everything about her is so much different from the women I work with and those parts of my pack. I can see why she wouldn't be as fond of my father and thus me — so many people associate me with him and rightly so. I am basically the guy's right-hand man. As the unsettling tension fades, a new tension fills the air — sexual. I watch as she bites her lips, and our undeniable magnetic attraction is begging for us to reconnect.

"Do you want to come to my place?" I ask nonchalantly, as I pay for the bill.

She only nods, as if saying yes would somehow betray her values. I must be such a forbidden subject for her... I am everything she stands against, and yet our bodies are calling to each other. After the valet pulls the car up and we're both buckled in, it's not long before our hands begin roaming.

She strokes my cock as it hardens beneath her touch. I groan, grateful for my shift senses. But still her touch is so divine, I almost have to pull over. It's all so distracting.

Her fingers delicately unzip my pants. "These windows are tinted, right?" she asks shyly.

I nod. It was against the law, of course, to have the front windows so deeply tinted... but one thing I learned at a young age is the laws don't apply when you're wealthy and a member of an elite society. Nette takes me in her mouth, licking and teasing my body, only picking up her speed when we'd reach a red light. Caressing her hair, she looks up at me briefly.

I both love and hate the red lights I keep hitting. They rewarded me with less teasing and a more fervent passion from Nette, yet they kept us from getting to my place sooner. And while I ache in sheer pleasure with each moment, I wanted nothing more than to do the same to her.

"Fuck, Nette," I plead with her at the next red light.

She giggles and goddamn, it's the hottest thing I've heard. "You're going to make me crash," I whisper.

"Shit. Really?" She pulls up, suddenly alert.

I burst out laughing. "We're almost there," I answer gruffly. "Keep going."

She licks her lips before going back down. Her eagerness, innocence, and passion all intrigue me deeply. I don't know her story, but I'll be damned if I won't find out. Because whoever Nette is, she is definitely not a reject. She is a goddess, and I will make her mine.

Chapter Five

Nette

I try not to let myself be consumed by the gorgeous and expansive house surrounding me. It's not hard as Noah drags me inside, guiding me upstairs and pushing me on top of his bed. He *is* strong. But so am I. Immediately propping myself back up, he pounces back on me, and wraps his forearm around my lower back, his free hand resting on my breast as he pulls me back into the kiss we started in the car.

All of my resolve is melting away and I feel myself growing weak at his touch, but it's different from last time. Instead of the drunken fevered rush, his movements are slow, tentative, as if he is searching my soul for the answers. I didn't share with him at dinner. As if he is already familiar with every inch of my body. He releases me from his lips, and I can barely catch my breath. My eyes searching his dark eyes for the answer to an unspoken question that he won't have the answers to — Is this okay? Is it okay for you to fuck the poor girl? For me to fuck the rich guy who is the embodiment of everything I fight against. Without the feverish rush, I long for him to dominate me, consumed by this feeling as if my body is being seen for the first time. A scar at the corners of his shoulder, and one tiny mole on his right cheek by his eyes, catch my attention. I suppose I am *seeing* him too. I note the golden flecks in his brown eyes and think they look like stars, a constellation I long to explore. I both love and hate the way I feel, completely naked under Noah's gaze. As if he sees all of my secrets — as if he can see how I was just hours before, in tears at my office, crying over my birth mother. Or the successes, failures, desires to defeat the men like his father. And he wants to be part of it all.

"Nette," he murmurs, guiding me to sit down on top of him, our bodies continue to face each other. He tucks a stray hair behind my ear. "You have the most beautiful eyes." He reaches for my hand; his thumb drawing circles inside the palm of my hand. "All of you is so fucking beautiful." He says this with so much conviction that I shiver under the power of words.

His passion is by far stronger than any self-doubt I have ever felt. As his fingers roam downward, sleeping under skies, my worries wash away under the holy water of what I choose to believe is truth. I am beautiful. I am divine. In this moment, I own this. At this moment, I belong.

This isn't how I would normally respond, but nothing about this feels normal — and thank God for that. It's bliss. Perfection. For a moment, the small voice in my head screams. This is too good to be true. Is he playing some sort of trick on me? But what does he have to earn from this? He could've let me run away the moment I stood up, but instead he kept me close. Pulling me down and using his witty banter and constant assurance to convince me to give him a chance. This is a new territory. I lean forward, my hips rocking against his fingers as they locate my clit.

My tongue glides across his ear lobe before nibbling at it. "You're not half bad yourself," I whisper.

His body shivers beside me. "Glad I swayed your opinion."

I can't help but smile, a new appreciation blossoming within me, which absolutely terrifies and delights me at the same time.

"Lay down." Noah commands, and there's an authoritative echo radiating in his voice. It's the same echo when he told me not to leave back at the restaurant. Back there, I didn't want to listen, but my body seemed to heed his command. Maybe it was a shifter thing - I have no idea. I've never been around my own kind until now.

But now I don't even hesitate. I instantly obeyed. "You're an alpha," I whisper, suddenly putting the pieces together.

"Not yet," he murmurs. As if he is afraid of what his next step will lead us, as if his commands would scare me. I nod at him to give him the go ahead. I want him to take over. I hate myself for it, but I do. I wish I could tell him that, but

I don't know how to put any of this into words. Least of all, when my body is begging for more, so I arch my hips up. Surely my body will show him. Slipping my skirt and panties down, he follows cues and reaches to remove my shirt.

Noah hovers his strong body over me. I start to unbutton his pants. "Mm," he moans.

He caresses my inner thigh as I start moving my hips to match the sweet circles. He draws over my clit. He slides in one finger and then two and my breast grows taut before he takes one in his mouth. With each suck and lick, he takes a break to breathe and sneaks a kiss on my neck and shoulders. I arch my hips higher, an invitation I long for him to notice, but he shushes me with a quick bite. "Patience, Nette."

Patience? "Fuck patience."

"You won't be fucking anything if you don't have some," he murmurs. "Trust me, Nette. This is killing me to be patient."

This was a new concept for me. Sucking my nipples, Noah picks up the speed of the delicious rhythm between his fingers and my clit. The build up to this point as every erogenous zone on my body more heightened than it's ever been, and fuck that look in his eyes when I murmured his name - it's all I can do not to beg. "Noah," breathless, I try to find my voice. "Do you think maybe we could... not be so... gentle... And um...... fuck?" My hips pick up speed, begging him to follow along, to increase his slow rhythm. He notes this switch in the pace and he tsks me.

"Now, now, love," he purrs. "Do you want me to stop?"

"No," I whimper. *Obviously not.* I reach my hands to search for his sex, gripping his hard-on, hoping to show him that it is okay to speed it up. To go rough. Even if I am savoring every minute of this — especially being sober. There is something so goddamn empowering in the way his body reacts, even if I'm not touching him.

"Dammit," he moans, ready to give in. "Are you sure you want this?"

I moan in response.

Chapter Six

Noah

She is a stubborn one, and I am so fucking glad I am just as stubborn. She pulls her free hand from my cock, gently grazing its way up to my lips. I kiss her fingertips. "You stop trying to prove yourself to me," I murmur, kissing the palm of my hand, and look back at her doe eyes.

"Proving myself?" she quips. "You've seen nothing yet."

I'm taken aback and surprised when she kneels down to take my length in her mouth. Again? This girl is so eager to please, and I love it. Her head bobbing eagerly, as if she could somehow sway me to give her what she was asking for. As if I have an agenda, despite not having one. I feel so completely enraptured by the eager passion lacing her hungry movements. I've half a mind to let her take exactly what she wants, but instead I pull back and flip her over. Alternating between teasing her clit and sliding my fingers deep inside, I wait until I am sure she is on the brink. Craving me more than she ever could, her body quivering. She arches her hips higher and says, "Noah. I need you."

I nod and stand up, walking away to a locked closet. Entering a code, I unearth my dark secret. A collection of toys, including whips, ropes, and handcuffs. I retrieved a toy I'm sure she'll enjoy and a sturdy rope. Silently, I straddled her, tying her hands to the posters of my bed. A wicked smile tugging at the corner of her lips. *Brat.* I toss the toy beside her, a device intended to suck her clit while I tend to the rest of her. As I slid in, I reached for the toy again, and placed the device in its desired location, as I picked up my speed, finally allowing her the rhythm I knew she was seeking.

Her scream echoes through the empty house.

"I know," I purr. "I knew you'd like this." My voice drips with satisfaction. I try another setting, increasing my own speed along with the power of the toy. Her body quaking relentlessly. She squeezes her hands, clearly frustrated not to have the freedom to guide me, digging her nails into me, but loving it, nonetheless. I begin grinding faster, deeper, only pausing to lick her neck, ears, and slap the side of her ass hard. She screams in delight. I'll have to use the whips next time, I note. She throws her legs around my back, using her strength and my body to take control to wildly bucking her hips in rhythm with mine.

I gasped.

"Noah!" she moans, her legs instantly shaking at the quick and fervent movements, the suction of the toy, and I follow suit, so overwhelmed by her own pleasure. Nette shakily tries to release her hands and lets out a growl when she remembers she can. My own free hand reaches above, grasping a fistful of her hair as I scream in ecstasy.

She lifts her hips up and begins rocking underneath the weight of my own. I just barely catch sight of her eyes rolling back and her lips trembling before I pull her hair. Her hands stop fighting the restraints, and she consumes all of my senses. Fuck, this woman will be the death of me. I know it with my entire being. But I can't stop, and I certainly don't want to. I can feel my claws breaking out and the sense of my shifter self-picking through the skin of my neck, and I can feel the same thing happening to her. The way her lips continue to tremble with each moan I elicit from her body, the closer and closer she gets.

"Noah," she murmurs, weak with desire. "I'm close." Her desperate voice leaves me on edge myself, so I bite down on her neck hard, holding myself back from my own release, waiting for her own pleasure to lead me to my climax. She doesn't notice how hard it is or she doesn't care, as she continues to lift her hips wildly faster than humanly possible. My tongue now licking the wound where I bit her, before allowing my body exactly what it was pleading for. My legs grow so weak — something I've never had to happen! I can barely keep the pace I want when she rips her hands free from the ropes restraining her and starts guiding my hips for me. "Noah, fuck, fuck, fuck!" It's not enough and finding my strength, I take control. Pulling her hair, I growl into her ear... Faster. More. Now. I feel her body tighten and spasm about me and I know I can't hold it back any long and neither can she. "I need this. I need you," she pleads. Her orgasm washes over us both and I finally find my own release with her, ready to collapse. But what kind of panther would I be if I stopped there? No, I tend to her as I watch one delicious wave after another wash over her taut body.

Speechless, both of us fall asleep after ravishing each other's bodies, and I can't help but wonder — have I found my mate? She may not be part of my pack, but she was a panther, and all partners technically belong to the Midnight Shadows Pack. I'll have to discover more than just her body and what makes her moan, I'll have to find out the truth about Nette. Because goddammit, does this woman make me feel things I've never felt.

I have dreams about her body, as if we both long for each other, even in another realm. I swear I can feel her soul wrapped tight around mine, as if her body is glued to me now. Strange. I blink in and out of consciousness, and I see her snuggled into me. A slight purr shivers through us when she pushes closer.

When I woke up at 3 AM, an unholy hour whispered about by my pack. I've never been much for superstition, but being giant black cats and all, my species has its fair share of lore. I look around though, and much to my horror, Nette is gone. There's not a single note. I ran around my house, frantically searching for her. It feels like the club all over again, my mysterious Cinderella of a woman. Thankfully, I have her number, and I expect to see a quick explanation from her when I open my phone. I don't.

I type out a quick I hope you're okay message and soon realize the normally blue text bubble is green. Either her phone is off, or she blocked me. A confusing mixture of emotions washes over me. Have I been a fool to jump so far ahead in thinking we had something more than just a one-nightstand? Perhaps. Perhaps I am getting a taste of my own medicine after all these years.

But Nette seemed so different. She *was* different. Different from any of the girls in my pack. Different from my co-workers. In contrast with Tessa. Different from even myself. She represented everything I longed to be, but never really could — not within the tight constraints my father always had over me.

And it hits.

Of course. Of course, that is exactly why she left. She made that clear the moment she knew who I was. Nette wanted nothing to do with the organization, the man — my father — that she was fighting against. With a heavy sigh, I push my feelings deep down to where they belong and lock them up once again. *Fool.*

I allow myself to drown once again in darkness — but still I can feel Nette's body beside me as I drift to sleep. Such a strange sensation. I awake to the sound of my alarm and make my way to work. My demeanor reflects more of my father's than usual, sending even the toughest of employees cowering. I hear whispers. "Now that he's CEO, he's gonna be a dick just like his dad." I wince, but maybe it's true. Maybe this is who I am meant to be. It's possible that Nette is correct. Maybe Tessa is right. Maybe I should just embrace this shit show.

Tessa gives me updates about my father's campaign and meetings I must attend as a new CEO, but it goes in through one ear and out the other. Instead, I look at her, wondering if I could get used to her being my mate. It's what my father wants. One day I'll be taking over as Alpha, so of course I'll need a mate, and if I can't have someone of substance, it might as well be Tessa. She's at least hot, and though I longed for so much more, it seemed this would have to do.

I look up at her with dark eyes, tilting my head, before stalking over to her. I pull her in for a deep kiss — a kiss I feel nothing as it happens. But I pretend I do by closing my eyes and imagining Nette's eyes instead. It's so easy, too. Since last night, it's as if something etched her into my skin and my mind.

Tessa pulls back breathlessly. "Took you long enough. I see your date didn't compare to yours truly, huh?"

I growl, my claws jutting out.

"Oh, calm down." She slams me onto my overpriced granite desk, something I realize Nette would absolutely hate.

With my eyes closed, I can imagine the thighs I caress belong to Nette. That it's her trembling under my touch. Not Tessa. I bite my lip to keep from uttering Nette's name. Tessa takes me into her mouth, but it's not her. It's Nette. We're back at my place and the events of last night play in a loop in my mind until my claws dig into my desk, and the crushing reality of what I've done engulfs me.

Chapter Seven

Nette

My body is still reeling from what happened just hours earlier when I tentatively make my way to what I assume is his shower. I feel like a fish out of water, trying to get this smart shower — who knew there were such things as smart showers — to spill out hot water and not cold. Finally, I figured it out. As I bathe myself with soaps and conditioners that I know cost more than my mother's rent. Grateful I didn't wake him up when I stepped out, I made my way downstairs, knowing I should leave soon.

I've already received two texts from my brother and ten from my mother. As I make my way through the kitchen and grab my purse where I dropped it, and rifle through it to find my purse to find my phone to request an Uber to pick me up.

"Going somewhere?"

I spin around and see someone who looks eerily like Noah but older, and when I realize who he is, I am amazed I didn't notice the resemblance sooner. "Mr. Kahan," I say. "I was just visiting your son." I blush.

"I know. I keep close tabs on him. I've been keeping close tabs on you, too. I didn't realize you'd made your way so close back home..."

I frown.

"Oh, yes, I know about you. Why do you think I fought so hard against the grant for your little charity project?"

A million ideas spin around in my mind. "Do you know my mother?" I ask.

"Yes."

My mouth drops.

"Oh, don't worry. There's no relation." He winks and I let out a sigh of relief. He reaches for an apple out of the bowl of fruit on the granite tabletops. They practically sparkle as if they are made of diamonds.

"I knew your father too," he continues. "But that's beside the point. Dear, I need to ask you something very important. If you can do this simple request for me, I can guarantee your family's safety. Both your birth family and those... creatures... you claim as your own. I will also contribute a generous amount to your little charity project."

My eyes brim with tears, because I know what's coming next. Of course, all of this would be too good to be true. But I want him to say it, so I just stand there silently.

"I want you to stop seeing my son. He can't have this kind of blemish on his reputation. He's a fool, so eager to branch out and be open, but he doesn't know where that can lead." He looks at me, clearly disgusted by my grandmother's dress, that I had so carefully picked out for the occasion. "You know where the rejects go. It's no life, am I right? Would you want that for Noah?"

"You promise my family will be safe?" I press, ignoring the mention of Noah entirely.

"Yes."

"I want a million dollars," I say, surprised at my bold request. A million dollars is a drop in the ocean for a man like Mr. Kahan, and it would go a long way for me and my family and the non-profit.

"A hundred thousand," he responds.

"I can stay here all day."

"And your family can die."

"And your son will know the truth about what a disgusting man you are."

"You're just like your father... Very well then."

I start to finish requesting my drive. "Don't worry. My driver will take you." I hesitate, but what choice do I have? This entire situation is a disaster. I followed Rob out to his Tesla and take a seat in the back with him. We make the drive-in silence to my side of town. All the while, I long to ask him about my mother and father, but I bite my tongue. I refuse to ask this man for anything more than necessary.

The lights are on in the living room when we get there, and I know my mother must be still waiting for me still. My heart sinks, wishing I had thought to text her, but how could I? The car door opens and as I step out, Rob calls out.

"Oh, and Nette, don't tell anyone about this. Not even your mother. As far as she is concerned, while you made a wonderful impression on us Kahan's and that is why we so generously donated to your organization, things simply did not work out between you and my son."

I nod and run inside. My mother and brother and a few of the other boarders are there. "We were so worried! You never don't answer your phone!" one of them cries out.

I nod, biting back my tears. "Yeah, it died, and I charged it on the Uber right here."

"That was a nice Uber!" my brother chimes in. "I figured it was you know who dropping you off."

"Ugh, Noah?" I summon my best impression of disgusting. "He was so boring. Talked about himself the entire time. I am so sorry for worrying all of you, but I am going to go rest."

Once I slip away to my room, I pull out my phone and immediately block Noah's number, figuring it would be the easiest option. A knock sounds at my door.

"Come in," I call out reluctantly.

"Honey," Mom says gently. "I've known you your entire life." She takes a seat beside my bed. "You were lying out there."

I nod. "I can't tell you the truth, okay?"

"Did he hurt you?"

"Noah? No."

She digests this information. "When you're ready, I am here to listen." I notice her hands are blue and shaking more than normal. A strange thought crosses my mind, one that chills me to the bone: *she won't be here for long*.

I pulled her into a deep hug. "Thank you."

"Always, hun."

Sucking in a deep breath, I decided to offer her one truth. "I think I'm going to try to find my birth parents."

She doesn't seem hurt by this. In fact, she seems happy. "I've been waiting for you to say that. Let me know how I can help."

"Thank you, Mom."

When I wake up in the morning, I see the generous million dollars sitting in the non-profit account. My brother eyes me suspiciously when he notices it. "Anything you'd like to share with the class today, Nette?"

I sigh. "Don't ask me, please."

He starts to pry more, but our mom shushes him. "Let her be. She's going through a rough breakup. I will say, that's a nice break up gift." She winks, but I can see the sadness in her eyes, begging to know what on earth I got myself into. I want to tell her I lost what could possibly be the best thing in my entire life, but I wouldn't know, because someone ripped it away before I could find out.

But we'll be safe. I just can't go after what is now forbidden to me. I must follow the demands of Mr. Kahan to keep us all safe — such a simple demand. Leave his son alone.

The rest of the day, everyone is squealing about the amount and what this means for us, and while I try to maintain a facade of happiness, I know everyone sees through it. I wish I could tell them — someone, anyone. The one time I need support and to be seen, I have to pretend nothing happened. And saying it was Noah, putting the blame on him, feels gross. My heart aches for Noah, and I can't help but wonder if he is hurting too — if my seemingly ghosting him impacted him at all.

The day goes by in slow motion.

And the day after that.

Until I lose all sense of time, wondering why I can't just be happy with what I have — my family and more than enough funds to help those who come to us for help.

I walk deep into the woods that lie on the outskirts of the city, feeling the cool breeze brush against my skin. I have always loved the feeling of the forest, the smell of the earth and the sounds of nature. I close my eyes and take a deep breath, feeling a sense of calm wash over her. *I needed this.*

As I open my eyes, I feel a tingling sensation in my body. I know what is about to happen. I have been suppressing my animal side for too long, and now it was demanding to be let out. The only time I was letting my claws bust out — literally and figuratively — was while I was with Noah. But now, that'll never happen again.

I looked around, making sure no one was nearby. I can't risk anyone to see me shift. Not because I am ashamed, but because the prejudices that exist against embracing your shifter side run deep. And it was even more taboo being who I am, a rare breed of elite shifters: a panther.

I closed my eyes once again and took another deep breath, focusing all my energy on the shift. At first my body refuses, whispering to me it knows we aren't allowed. "It's okay," I whisper back to myself. "We are safe here."

Safe. Something I've longed for. I am safe with my family, but even they frown on adults shifting for fun. I feel it in my bones as they crack and reshape themselves, my muscles bulging as fur sprouts all over her body. I open my eyes and look down, seeing my paws instead of my feet. Finally, I breathe.

I stretch my legs and take a few steps, feeling the power of my panther form. I dig my paws into the ground for a second before I start to run, leaping over fallen logs and dodging between trees. It is such a feeling of pure freedom, a release of all the stress that had been building up inside me. Nothing exists but me and nature.

I ran for a while until I reached a small clearing in the woods with a tiny creek. Sitting down by the rustling water, I look up at the sky, feeling the warmth of the sun on my fur. It is a rare moment of peace, a chance to reflect on everything that has been happening in my life.

To call things difficult would be an understatement. And once Noah popped up in my life, my entire world was shattered. The encounter with his father? In the forest's peace, I can finally admit I am torn. Part of me says I need to tell him the truth. I know if my mother knew the truth, she'd tell me that's exactly what I should do. But if I do, that could put my family in danger. I have to protect them at all costs, even if it means keeping secrets on all sides.

Taking a deep breath, I let myself bask in the sun's warmth on my aching soul, knowing it too will be leaving me, as I watch it finish setting behind the trees. I consider what it will look like if I do what I know my mother would expect me to do. After all, how can I accept dirty money and let anyone else control my life?

But I know how. I know we have to do what we have to. Simple as that.

I smile as the stars peek out, and memories of my brothers shifting into wolves in these very woods light up my mind... They used to shift with me all the time, but now that we are all older, they saw it as childish and risky. They had moved on to other things, like helping their mother with running the non-profit and what seemed like a never-ending search to find mates. But I never could let go of the feeling I get when I shift. It's so similar to being with Noah. Raw. Real. It is a part of who I am, and though I hide it often, I refuse to let anyone take that away from me.

My eyes blink open once again and I stand tall, my body cracking back into place and my fur retracting as my smooth skin accepts the greeting of moonlight. I am cleansed with a renewed sense of strength. I know what I have to do. As hard as it is, I have to let Noah go. I have to pretend like none of this ever happened and simply enjoy the financial rewards of being blackmailed. I take one last look at the moonlit-dappled forest around me, and then walk back to where I left my clothes.

Once dressed, I find myself back in town, driving down the familiar poverty-stricken streets that hold more kindness than the rich elite panther shifters she should belong to. "I am grateful," she whispers, realizing for once, she is grateful that her birth mother dropped her off at that door all those nights ago. Whatever the reason, selfish or not, she is glad. In another life, she wouldn't have such a sense of purpose. I wouldn't be able to help the people I help.

I heard a loud cry in the middle of the night, and I bolted instantly. It's only been a week since my encounter with Noah's father, and I've done everything he's asked. Even my mother doesn't know the truth, but all I can think is that he has changed his mind and has sent his men after my family, anyway. I make my way to the source of the noise alongside my brother and the other boarders, which leads us to my mother's room.

"Oooh!" she cries out. "Call 911!"

I fumble for my phone, dropping it, and my brother picks it up, taking control while I sit beside her. "Oh mama, what is it?"

She does her best to state she thinks it's a heart attack calmly, but I can see the fear flash across her features. I held her hands until the paramedics got there and whisked her away, my brother and I following quickly behind. Can things get any worse?

As if on cue, the Universe decides to answer that question. Inside the emergency room waiting room sits none other than Noah, bloodied and bruised, with wide eyes. The moment he sees me, he runs up to me, tears in his eyes. "How did you know?"

I blink. "Know what?"

He looks around, confused.

"My mom had a heart attack," I explain coolly, fighting everything in me that begged for his touch to comfort me, everything that wanted to make sure he was also okay.

Chapter Eight

Noah

"Fuck being Alpha!" I snap.

"Well, you need to fuck something. It sounds like you did have a little moment with Tessa today." He sips his coffee. "Office gossip is always such a delight."

I sigh. "Look, I am not going to be with Tessa. What happened in my office — and can I say how disturbing it is that you know what happened — anyway, it's not happening again!"

"Well, it's probably for the best. Why would Tessa or any respectable shifter want you?"

The words sting. A truth that's been playing on repeat in my head since Nette ghosted me. "You don't know that." I comment weakly.

"Nette? She clearly didn't want anything to do with you. Why are you hung up over a random bitch when you have the likes of Tessa fawning over you? Goddamn, son, you aren't even fit to be a CEO. Let alone an Alpha. What am I going to do when it's time for me to pass on the torch?"

My claws dig into my fists as I throw a punch at my father.

He pulls back and laughs. "Well, shit." He wipes his jaw that's now pooling blood. "Maybe you do have some Alpha in you after all."

I let out a low laugh.

Before I know it, searing pain burns my face and my entire body as my dad rakes his claws against my skin. "You lay a hand on me again, son. You will regret it."

"I can't believe I just got in a fistfight with my own father!" I shout on the phone, expecting my mother to show some form of empathy, only she doesn't. How foolish could I be? Tessa sits beside me, rubbing circles on my back, which only annoys me further. Doesn't she know she's part of the reason we got into this fight? *Dammit.*

I reach for my glass of bourbon, the dark liquid promises to soothe my pain. "I'm sure he'll be home soon," I comment, when my mom asks when my dad left.

Tessa tries yet again to soothe me. She has been trying to get into my pants ever since we made out last week before my father interrupted us, much to his disappointment, but I couldn't even get hard, so it was a grateful escape.

"Why did you two even fight?" she asks, pulling away.

"You."

She brightens. "Oh?"

"It's not what you think," I snap.

"Oh..."

"I let him know I wouldn't be choosing you as my mate under any circumstances. He was.... displeased. By that and my 'hang up' on some random chick who ghosted me."

"That Nette girl?" she asks, annoyed. "Wait. Is that why you finally tried to fuck me?"

I nod, completely oblivious to Tessa's tears. "My father said I wasn't fit to be an Alpha, let alone a CEO. All because I don't wanna take you fake bitches as a mate."

Tessa grabs my bottle of bourbon from the table before smashing it against my already injured cheek. "Tell your dad I agree."

Goddamn it! I would be mad, but she is right. And as annoying and crazy as she is, I deserved this. My words crossed a line. I know that. "Tess," I call out. "I am sorry. Okay?"

She is storming down the hall, and I know chasing after her will only worsen the situation. At this point, I'm going to need stitches even with my healing capabilities. If everyone keeps hitting the same spot, it's never going to heal.

The thought catches me — and I wonder if that's why I am so broken, so different from the rest of those in my pack.

I couldn't tell my father that Tess shared his sentiments because moments after it happened my mother was calling me again. "Your father has been in a car accident. It's serious."

Serious. For a shifter. This is bad.

I rushed to the emergency room. I am only there for what can be five minutes. My mother and the others haven't even arrived yet. When I see the only person I want to see in this moment burst through the doors like an angel. My savior. *Nette.*

I rushed up to her. "How did you know?"

"Know what?"

And I realized that she wasn't there for me. I released her body from my awkward embrace, realizing she was stiff in it. *What happened?* When she mentions her mother is here for a heart attack, I notice a young man and a few others follow behind her. "Oh," I say, standing tall and doing my best to be the asshole she perceives me to be. "Good luck with that."

She sighs, and her body seems to slouch in response. My heart aches. I want to hold her. Soothe her pain. But no... she thinks I'm evil. Everyone thinks I am lacking in one way or another. I might as well start living up to it all.

She starts to turn and walk away when she spins around. "Wait. Why are you here? What happened to you?" She examines my face, my wounded cheek.

"My dad. We got into a fight." I explain, opting to leave out that some injuries came from Tessa.

"About me?" she asks, shocked.

"About you?" I reply with equal surprise. "Why would we fight about you?"

She hesitates. "I don't know, sorry. That was a dumb assumption."

Before I can question her further, her family dragged her away. "Nette, the doctor is asking for us." My heart jumps and I say a silent prayer that her mother is okay, before I too find myself being called back by a nurse. When I get there, I note my father is barely scathed. "I thought this was bad?" I glared at him. "What kind of game are you playing?"

"I am making a point. I can be gone at any moment, and you need to be ready to take over my legacy. And I can't have some weak little bitch, be the one to do that."

"Then pick another heir!"

"You are my only heir!" he growls.

"Well, that must be sad for you to have a son like me." I sit down, realizing my wounds from our fight and Tessa's attack are far worse than his minor scratches are. I think back to my encounter with Nette, and it seems so far-fetched, but I have to ask. "Did you say something to Nette?"

"Who?"

"Nette. The girl you think I am so dumb for being hung up on."

"No. I don't even know her. Why would you think that?"

"Because I can't seem to understand why she stopped talking to me for no reason…"

My dad interrupts, "You're being paranoid, son."

"You literally just faked an entire car accident, having Mother call me that it was bad." No wonder she wasn't here — she must've known his intentions. "I think if anyone is paranoid or overreacting, it's you."

"I am only doing what is best for this family. For the pack. Girls like Nette, they don't belong mixed with our kind."

I frown. "She is one of our kind."

"Is she?" he laughs. "She's a panther, sure, but she's not in our pack. Did you know that she stands up for the weak? She fights for shifters who are not of our kind, shifters who give the rest of us a bad name."

I didn't know enough about Nette outside of her body to know all the things she does in her life, but dammit, that doesn't sound like a bad thing. In fact, her fighting for the 'weak' intrigues me all the more. "What did you say to her? When did you say something to her?" I ask.

"I told you. I didn't say anything."

"Tell me the truth." I growl. "Now."

"Son, she was paid well for her space and silence. Let it go."

Paid? Nette left me for money? That made no sense. "What else did you do?"

He laughed. "I may have threatened the safety of her family."

"You didn't have anything to do with her mother's hospital visit, did you?"

He frowns. Before I can react, the doctor walks in to discuss treatment with my father, and I leave the room.

I beg to see Nette, but the nurses say they can't confirm if she or her mother are there, even if I know she is. I waited hours, my dad had already been discharged. My phone silenced — after twenty calls from Tessa, I couldn't bear to look at it anymore. Finally, one of the men that came in with Nette walks out. "Hey! You were with Nette." I pause, hoping he's not a new boyfriend. "Is she... Is her mom okay?"

"Our mom is okay," he answers. "You're Noah, right?"

I nod.

Before I know it, the man is placing a fist right in front of my face. A nurse screams out. "It's okay!" I call out, waving my hand dismissively. "I'm sure I deserved it. Kind of." *I really am going to need those stitches at this rate.*

"I don't know what happened between you two, but you broke her." He breathes. "So, it's kind of my duty as a brother."

"I respect that."

He holds out his hand. "Lawrence. The older and less attractive version of me in the corner there is Angel."

"Nice to meet you."

"I'll let my sister know you're still here."

"Can you tell her I know my dad tried to keep her away from me?" I ask.

His jaw drops. "Now that's the tea!"

After a few minutes, Nette walks out with tears in her eyes and a big smile. "You figured it out?" As soon as she says it, her heart drops. "Wait, does that mean I am in danger?"

I sigh, pulling her into a tight hug. "We'll figure out the details later, but right now, you're safe. How is your mom?" I paint on a solid face of cool assuredness, because I know my father never backs down from a promise. Or a threat.

"She's okay. We're lucky we caught it quickly. They gave her some medicine, and she is gonna be okay!" Tears fill her eyes. "I was so scared!"

"You've been here for hours," I note. "Can I take you away for a bit?"

She breathes. "Yes. I think I'd like that."

In the car, tears start pooling, and I wonder if perhaps I made another mistake. "Nette?"

"It's nothing... I just... I am glad you're here. I'm glad I don't have to go through this alone."

I held her hand. "I won't let you go through any of this alone."

She squeezes my hand in response, and as her tears dry, her hands explore my body. She gently grazes my cheek. "I'm sorry about my brother. He told me he kind of punched you."

"Well, at least he punched me in the same spot as everyone else. It should heal soon."

"Everyone else? I thought it was just your dad..."

"It's a long story," I confess.

"You've taken one too many hits in my name."

"Well, I have an idea about how you can make that up to."

"Mm?" she perks up. "I have an idea, too."

Yet again, I find myself in the mouth of a woman as I speed down a freeway, eager to get to my home. Eager to explore a body I am now growing more and more familiar with. She teases me and keeps me just at the edge before pulling back. I drive faster, my shifter sense keeping us both safe.

As soon as I see lights flashing behind me, I know I've made a mistake. I shouldn't have taken the freeway. "Sit up, Nette." I command.

She obeys and sees the lights too. I zip my pants and she wipes her lips as I pull over. "Don't worry. We won't get in trouble. Once I flash my ID, they'll let it go..."

"Is there a reason you're speeding?"

"I am so sorry. My name is Mr. Kahan. My father was in a horrible car accident." My stomach twists at the lie that is also somehow the "truth" to those on the outside.

"I heard on the news Rob was taken to the hospital..."

"Which should be all the more reason I should be careful, I know... but I was just so stressed, and my girlfriend and I were heading back to my place to get some things to stay with my dad overnight."

He nods. "I understand. I do have to let you know these tinted windows are illegal... Also, drive slower, okay?"

As I hit the gas and make my way back on the freeway, Nette laughs. "I can't believe you are everything I hate, yet here I am. In the palm of your hands."

I smile. "There might be more to me than you think."

Somehow, our clothes fall off before we even make our way through the door, our bodies needing the comfort of each other. We make it to the sofa before I wrap her legs around my shoulders and take her into my mouth, licking her clit and teasing her, sliding my fingers in and out, her body quaking in release. "Noah!" Our bodies fall back into a familiar rhythm as I climb on top, sliding inside her until we both find our release.

I briefly recall my plans of using my whip in our next encounter, glad it seems we'll have plenty of "next encounters" to come.

We may have our own separate worlds against us, but at this moment all we have is each other and those worlds melt away. Her hips lifting eagerly underneath me, our claws breaking through, digging into each other. I don't know the answers or how we'll make it through this, but we will.

We have to.

As we collapse into each other, she looks up at me, her eyes wide with passion. "I thought I'd never have this again. Is that lame to admit?"

I laugh. "Not lame at all. I was afraid of the same thing," I confess.

She blinks, as if processing this truth took a great deal of effort. I leaned forward, much to my own surprise, and gently kissed her forehead. "I know," I whisper. "I am surprised too."

"How are we going to make this work?" she asks.

"Step one, let's not worry about what this is." I speak. "Let's just live in this moment, okay?"

She nods. "I think I can live with that."

Standing up, I grab her wrists and pull her up. "Nette, let's go back to my room, shall we?"

She raises her brow. "Again?"

"I had something in my closet I think you'd like to... experience."

She giggles and whatever this is, I can't wait to explore the depths of it.

Of her and our so-called forbidden romance.

Chapter Nine

Nette

I drift off to sleep, processing the chaos of the last few days, holding onto Noah's guidance to live in the moment. For now. I worry about my mother and my family and what all of this will mean for us. For my pack. For the nonprofit. But I let myself forget, for just a moment — and I let Noah's arms wrap around me, a promise of a lullaby that can keep me safe, even if it's just an illusion.

"It'll be okay," he murmurs, as if sensing this shift in my energy.

"I know," I whisper. "I know."

As the sun peeks through the windows, the aroma of freshly baked biscuits and sausage gravy fill the bedroom, pouring in through the vents... Noah must've woken up early to cook.

I make my way downstairs and back into the kitchen, where I last saw Noah's father the night he blackmailed me into staying away from one who could be the best person to happen in my life. Stepping into the kitchen, and the sight of the delicious breakfast makes my stomach grumble. I am absolutely famished!

My heart warms with thoughtful gestures — it's all from scratch, I notice. The pile of flour that must've spilled on the floor is my first clue. I can't help but smile when I see Noah in his cooking apron, his hair a mess, and flour dusting his cheeks.

"This smells amazing!" I exclaim, giving him a warm hug.

"Thanks," Noah replies, beaming with pride. "It's my grandma's recipe. I used to spend Sundays with her, and she would always make this for me."

His face softens as he continues to speak of his grandma. It's sweet, and I listen intently as Noah shares his memories of his grandma. I can see the love and fondness he had for her, and this new and raw side of Noah makes my heart swell. Perhaps he is more than the guy I assume him to be. More than just a rich and elite figure basking in privilege.

As I bite into the delicious meal, I shower Noah with compliments. "It would impress my mom by how authentic these are!" I almost tear up, thinking of my mom and how I almost lost her. What would I have done? What if last night went differently? It felt like so many pieces lined up for us to be here right now. Be here and safe.

"My mom has always been there for me," I confess. "It killed me to not tell her about us and what happened. The idea of losing her too? I was so scared. My mom took me in when I was abandoned as a baby, but she never treated me any differently. She loved me as if I was her very own. I will always be grateful for her love and support."

As they finished their meal, Noah held me in his gaze, his eyes full of longing and tenderness. It sends a shiver throughout my entire body.

"Not all of my family is horrible and scary," he adds softly. "There are some good ones out there, like my grandma."

I nod, feeling saddened by his need to justify his family to me. I can't imagine having such a cruel father as Mr. Kahan. "I am sure your grandmother is lovely."

I lean in and kiss him, savoring the last moments before we must face the reality of his father. At the moment, I know I have found someone special, someone who shares my deepest desires.

Our kiss blooms and soon Noah is swiping the items off the table, placing me on top as the glasses around us shatter. He takes my breast in his mouth, whispering something about never getting used to feasting on my body, but I'm too wrapped up by the sensations to decipher it. He licks my tits, sucking and teasing me in a slow, torturous way that should be a crime. In agonizing minutes, his tongue trails down to my hips. He kisses my hips, my thighs, and stomach before taking me into his mouth. I gasp — and I know I will never get used to him feasting on me, either.

My hips arch, following the rhythm of his tongue as he puts his hands under my ass, my legs wrapped around his head. He lifts both of us upward, continuing to devour me.

"Dammit, Noah," I moan, both thrilled with his teasing nature and frustrated all at the same time. He pulls back and orders me once again to be patient.

I laugh, repeating the same line as before. "Fuck patience." I giggle as he carries me upstairs to his room. Laying me gingerly on this bed, he pulls out the whip he's promised to tease me with. I eagerly arch my ass up, but he only grazes me with the braided rope.

"Touch yourself with the same caress as this whip," he orders, and I comply without hesitation. Stroking my clit slowly, gently. He whips my ass and I let out a yelp, realizing this is my cue to pick up my speed. Circling more, applying more pressure, he whips me again a few more times. "Fuck," I cry out. Each smack heightens my sense of pleasure. The closer I get, the more frequent the whips get, before Noah stops and picks me up once again, flipping me over to climb on top of me.

He enters my body while taking my breast in his mouth once again. My hips with a mind of their own ride against me, as I grip a fistful of his air. Some part of me is screaming for him to never leave, but I don't dare let the words escape my lips. But somehow, I know, this feeling is starting to bud at this moment. This is where it starts, I think. Where passion blurs into something else, something I am scared I'll never be able to hold.

His hips crash into mine even more fervently. "Fuck!" he groans, his nails breaking through as they dig into the headboard. I bite his shoulder, my teeth gliding out. I've never felt so safe to explore my animalistic side, but that is the thing about Noah.

He is safe.

I dig my teeth deeper and he groans in that beautiful mix of pleasure and pain. All the lines seem to blur when we're together, and now the lines, much like our bodies, melt into each other with a need we can only fulfill in each other. I cry out his name as my body shivers along with his own spasms.

He rolls over, catching his breath. I giggle and ask him. "Are you going to make us lunch now?"

He catches his breath. "We can order in."

"Oh?"

"Don't think I was going to let you out of my sight anytime soon," he quips.

"About that..." I look up at him, the worry from earlier seeping back in.

"I promise. I will protect your family from my father at all costs."

He says the words so firmly; I don't doubt him. Not for a second. At this moment, I know I am choosing this. Whatever it is. Even if all the cards are stacked against us and we come from different worlds. I've wanted nothing more. Much like patience, forbidden love, be damned!

Acknowledgments

A special "Thank You" to all of you who take the time to read my work.

With Love
Phoenix Skyy

ALSO BY

PHOENIX SKYY

Diva Crazy in Love

Because of You

Forbidden Series (1 - 3)

ALSO BY

MIND FLOW PUBLISHING

The Mary B Chronicles (1- 4)

The Freedom in the Cage Series (1 - 4)

Finding Kate

A Chance at Love

Split Decision

Sophie's Pack

Mental Interlude

Spoken From the Heart

Simple Complexity

Falling in Love With Poetry

Charisma's Homecoming

www.ingramcontent.com/pod-product-compliance
Lightning Source LLC
LaVergne TN
LVHW040106080526
838202LV00045B/3792